Anonymous

Memorial of John Willard, LL. D.

Consisting of addresses and notices on the occasion of his death, and in

illustration of his life and character. Collected for the gratification of his

friends

Anonymous

Memorial of John Willard, LL. D.
Consisting of addresses and notices on the occasion of his death, and in illustration of his life and character. Collected for the gratification of his friends

ISBN/EAN: 9783337402990

Printed in Europe, USA, Canada, Australia, Japan

Cover: Foto ©Raphael Reischuk / pixelio.de

More available books at **www.hansebooks.com**

Memorial

OF

JOHN WILLARD, LL. D.

FORMERLY

CIRCUIT JUDGE AND VICE CHANCELLOR OF THE FOURTH CIRCUIT, AND
AFTERWARDS JUSTICE OF THE SUPREME COURT AND A MEMBER
OF THE SENATE OF THE STATE OF NEW YORK;

CONSISTING OF

ADDRESSES AND NOTICES

ON THE OCCASION OF HIS DEATH, AND

IN ILLUSTRATION OF HIS LIFE AND CHARACTER.

Collected for the gratification of his friends.

SARATOGA SPRINGS:
STEAM PRINTING PRESSES OF G. M. DAVISON.
1863.

CONTENTS.

...

HON. JOHN WILLARD.

The following announcement of the death of Hon. John Willard, appeared in the *Saratogian*, September 4, 1862:

DEATH OF JUDGE WILLARD.

It is with feelings of deep regret that we are called upon to announce the death of Honorable John Willard, who expired at his residence in this village, on Sunday, the 31st day of August last. The disease with which he suffered was paralysis of the right side, which in the space of twelve days carried him off. Though for several months past he has been in feeble physical strength, yet he possessed the mental vigor and elasticity of a ripe manhood.

Although in a period like this of great national excitement and peril, the loss of an individual however exalted in position and merit, seems to attract less attention than in ordinary times, yet the death of Judge Willard has spread great sorrow over the hearts of the people of this state.

For more than forty years he has filled offices of high honor and public trust with signal ability and integrity. A profound jurist, a ripe scholar and a man of rare decision of character, he possessed a modest and retiring disposition, which required an intimate acquaintance to fully appreciate his worth and excellence. His private life was singularly pure and blameless, and among his friends in the social circle his kindness, his conversational powers backed by a great fund of general information, made intercourse with him delightful and instructive.

He was born on the 20th day of May, 1792, at Guilford, Connecticut, and graduated at Middlebury College, in August, 1813. While at college he was associated with the late Silas Wright and Hon. Samuel Nelson, and evinced at that time the same patriotic solicitude for the success of his country while engaged with a foreign power, that has since shone so conspicuous during the progress of the present treasonable rebellion. He was admitted to practice as an attorney of the Supreme Court in 1817, under the Chief Justiceship of Smith Thompson, and entered upon the practice of the law in Salem, Washington county. Bringing to the profession of his choice a well-stored and disciplined mind, he soon attained, by his untiring industry, and without any adventitious aid, an enviable eminence in his profession. He was for many years first Judge of the Common Pleas, and Surrogate of Washington Co., until in 1836, on the elevation of Esek Cowen to the bench of the Supreme Court, he was appointed Circuit Judge and Vice Chancellor of the Fourth Judicial District, filling that office until the new organization of the Judiciary under the constitution of 1846, when he was elected one of the Justices of the Supreme Court. This latter office he held until 1854; and under the regulations of our judicial system, was a member of the Court of Appeals during the last year of his term of service. The rapidity and ability with which he discharged his judicial duties; his uniform courtesy and kindness to the profession; and above all, the pureness and integrity of his character, as a judge and as a man, commanded universal respect and esteem, and won for him many flattering testimonials of regard from the bar in the different counties of this district.

After his retirement from the bench he was engaged for some years in the preparation of several legal treatises, which are valuable contributions to our jurisprudence, and not less distinguished for felicity and perspicuity of style than accurate and profound legal research and learning.

As a politician he was attached to the Democratic party, and strong and decided in his political opinions; but, upon the breaking out of the present wicked and causeless rebellion, he sunk the partizan in the patriot, and took early and strong grounds in favor of a united support to our government in its struggle with treason.

In 1861 he was the candidate of the Union Convention for Senator, and subsequently endorsed by all other parties, he was elected without opposition. While in the Senate he uniformly acted with the Union Democrats and Republicans, and his opinion on all questions before that body was received with great respect. By his efforts the confusion in the laws respecting murder, and the rights of married women, was removed, and simple and sensible statutes passed in relation thereto.

As an advocate, a judge, a legislator, he was alike eminent and accomplished ; and in his private life irreproachable and blameless. It has fallen to the lot of few men to acquire and leave behind them such an honorable and unsullied name.

He lived to bury his only child in 1853, and his estimable wife in 1859 ; and cut off thus from his family ties, his great heart turned with affection and solicitude to the welfare of his country. The troubles and perils of the present crisis caused him great anxiety and care, and evidently wore upon his health and strength.

He was buried from his residence, on Wednesday afternoon, and a devout and consistent christian, he has gone to the rewards which await the pure in spirit, the blameless in life and the upright in heart.

RESOLUTIONS

𝔅ar of 𝔖aratoga 𝔖prings,

CONTAINING

ADDRESSES OF WM. L. F. WARREN, R. H. WALWORTH, A. BOCKES,
O. L BARBOUR, JUDIAH ELLSWORTH, JOSEPH A.
SHOUDY, AND JAMES P. BUTLER.

A meeting of the members of the Bar, of Saratoga Springs, called for the purpose of expressing the feelings of the profession on the death of their lamented brother, was held on the 2d day of September, 1862. Hon. W. L. F. WARREN was appointed chairman, and JOHN L. BARBOUR, secretary.

On taking his seat the CHAIRMAN made the following remarks :
‹ Gentlemen : Death has again been in our midst, and one of our respected and beloved citizens has become its victim. Unrelenting in his pursuit, the fell destroyer often lingers on our pathway, and by insidious advances marks his object with unerring certainty ; but too often he comes at a day and hour we think not.

The Hon. JOHN WILLARD has been unexpectedly stricken down at the end of a long life ; but it may be said, in the midst of his honors, and usefulness. The deceased had reached the allotted period of three score years and ten ; but they were not years of inactivity. The fruits of a highly cultivated intellect, disciplined by early habits of industry and experience, and enriched by an extensive acquaintance with legal precedents, and varied literary attainments, bloomed and blossomed even in his old age. The results of his cultivated mind, which gave eminence to the judicial position, which he held for more than a third of a century, did not terminate with his public career. His retirement to private life was occupied principally in the preparation of several volumes of legal treatises, which have been completed and given to the public, and which are not less creditable to his genius and learning, than useful to the profession.

My first acquaintance with the deceased was as early as 1817, when we mutually became members of a class examined for admission to practice as attorneys of the supreme court. He commenced the practice of the law in the county of Washington. After some years of successful practice in the profession, he was appointed successively to the offices of surrogate and judge of that county, the duties of which he fulfilled with great ability for about twenty years. Subsequently he accepted the office of circuit judge and vice chancellor of the fourth circuit, which event led him to change his place of residence to this village, where he continued to exercise the duties of those offices until they terminated, and were succeeded by the present organization of the courts of this state. Under this new organization he was elected a judge of the supreme court for the term of eight years; serving the last year of the term in the court of appeals. With his service of one year in the latter court, his judicial career terminated. In the fall of the year 1861 he was elected to represent this district in the senate of this state, in which office his distinguished efforts in sustaining the government, commanded the approval of his constituents, and added new laurels to his abilities as a statesman.

This is not the time or occasion to dwell on the gifted qualities of mind and character possessed by the deceased. His judicial opinions, scattered through numerous volumes, well known to the profession, furnish an enduring monument to his learning and ability as a judge; and the social circle he was wont to delight by his presence and conversation, bear witness to the many virtues which marked his intercourse in private life.

The deceased was a true christian gentleman, not only in name and by profession, but in practice. He was an exemplary member, in communion with the Presbyterian church of this village for many years, and all who knew him can testify to the purity and benevolence of his life and character. He will no longer move among the throngs of the living; but his memory will be cherished for his exalted qualities as a judge and senator—for his patriotism, liberality and genial intercourse as a citizen, and for his urbanity, kindness and sympathy as a friend and benefactor. The occasion is a solemn admonition to us who survive him. Let it be our resolve "*dum vivimus vivamus*," and by emulating his many excellencies and virtues, may we be prepared to inherit his immortality.

The chairman appointed the following gentlemen a committee on resolutions: John Newland, Hon. A. Bockes, T. G. Young, H. W. Merrill, J. W. Crane, Waldo M. Potter.

The following resolutions were reported by John Newland, Esq., chairman of the committee, and unanimously adopted:

Whereas, The members of the Bar in this village, in common with the rest of the community, have received with poignant sorrow the announcement of the decease of the Hon. John Willard, which occurred on the 31st day of August last, and have met to give an expression to their sense of the loss which they as individuals, as well as members of the legal profession, have sustained in this afflictive dispensation, we do now record with emotions of gratitude to God, mingled with grief at our own loss,—

First. That the eminent jurist, whose recent death we mourn, was gifted with a peculiarly clear and powerful intellect, quick and elevated moral perceptions, generous sympathies, and a sound judgment which made him an ornament to his profession, and especially fitted him to fill with honor and usefulness high judicial positions — that he has left in several masterly works a monument of his legal learning and literary abilities, which greatly enhances his claim to the homage of his brethren.

Second. That in his long public career he exhibited a degree of devotion to his official duties, of purity of purpose, unbending integrity and ardent patriotism, which secured to him the confidence, respect and admiration of the people whom he served, and will embalm his name in their hearts.

Third. That in the walks of private life he was distinguished by the simplicity of his manners, the modesty of his demeanor, the tenderness of his sympathies, and the consistency and purity of his christian character.

Therefore it is resolved:

1. That in the death of Judge Willard the judiciary and bar have lost a distinguished ornament, the state a judicious, safe and diligent legislator, this village a kind, liberal and enlightened citizen, and the whole country a fervent, self-sacrificing patriot.

2. That while thus indicating the public nature of this dispensation, we do not forget that it has reached individual hearts, upon whose grief we do not venture to intrude further than to tender to them our warmest sympathy, and to remind them that their deceased friend, having lived honorably and usefully and died in the christian hope which he had cherished for many years, their loss is his infinite gain.

3. That as a mark of respect to the memory of our lamented friend, we will in a body attend his funeral.

4. That a copy of this minute and these resolutions, signed by the chairman and secretary, be presented to the relatives of the deceased, and that the same be published in the several papers of this village.

CHANCELLOR WALWORTH said he had been acquainted with our lamented brother, Judge Willard, for about fifty years, having become acquainted with him when the judge was in college at Middlebury. From the time the judge was admitted to the bar, although four years his senior, down to the day of his death, he had been intimately acquainted and on terms of friendship with him. As a lawyer it might truly be said of him *semper paratus, semper fidel's;* for he was always ready and prepared to argue the cause of his client when the time arrived for him to do so ; and no lawyer ever discharged that duty more faithfully and honorably. And during the long period of nearly thirty years that he occupied a judicial station as county judge and vice chancellor, justice of the supreme court, judge of the court of appeals, and as a judge of the court for the trial of impeachments, no judicial officer ever discharged his official duties more uprightly or more faithfully. Indeed, such was my confidence in his capacity and his sound discretion as a county judge, when he was first appointed to that office, and when I was presiding in the court of oyer and terminer, that I requested him to take the whole management of the trial of a capital case. And to those who were afterwards acquainted with him as a judge, it is needless to say that at that early day my perfect confidence in his capacity to discharge the most important of all judicial duties, was not misplaced. Indeed, as a lawyer and a judge, he is a pattern and an example to be followed by all our younger brethren who desire to obtain eminence and honor in the profession. But especially would I recommend to my brethren of the law to follow the example of our deceased friend as an honest, upright christian gentleman, in all the social and private relations of life. For a more upright man in all the varied relations of life I have never known. And long will his memory be cherished, not only by his immediate relatives, but by all who have known him and appreciated his virtues as I have.

Hon. A. BOCKES said :

Mr. Chairman : I cannot refrain from making a few observations on this melancholy occasion, although, with me, it requires an effort to speak of those for whom I mourn. It has been said that it is not by words that the living pay to the dead the sincerest and most eloquent tribute. I feel that it is so, and will therefore occupy your attention but for a moment.

The death of Judge Willard has cast a gloom over all classes of this community. He had lived so long among us and so familiarly that all knew him and esteemed him as a true man and faithful friend. His death has produced general lamentation among our citizens. Conscious that he has departed from among us, we feel desolate and subdued. This common sentiment of our community affords a touching tribute to his worth. It speaks of his kindness—of his affection—of his sympathy—of his generosity.

But I do not purpose, on this occasion, to draw attention to the various phases of his admirable character—only to echo the wail of sorrow which floats around us in stifled murmurs. I cannot now, if I would, command the appropriate words of eulogy. I can only say that a great and good man has fallen in our midst—not in youth, nor in the meridian of his years, but ripe in time and in honors—"The thread of his life is cut; the immortal is separated from the mortal; and the products of a great and cultivated mind are all that remain to us of the jurist and legislator."

O. L. BARBOUR said:

Mr. Chairman: We meet on this occasion to attempt some expression of our sentiments on the death of one of our most distinguished citizens. The Hon. John Willard—*clarum et venerabile nomen*—a man venerable for his years, eminent in his profession, and estimable for his many virtues, is no more. It is fit and proper that we, members of his own profession, who have witnessed the manner in which he has adorned that profession; that we, his neighbors, who have sat at his feet and imbibed lessons of wisdom and virtue from his lips, and who have known the beauty, the simplicity and the integrity of his daily life, should give utterance, ere the grave closes over his remains, to the emotions which overwhelm us. We owe it to the memory of him who has gone, that some tribute—feeble though it be—should be paid to his memory; that some record should be made of our feelings as a class, and as individuals. We owe it also to the younger members of the bar, and to those who are to come after us, that so bright an example as that of Judge Willard should not be allowed to die out and be forgotten, when we, who have had personal knowledge of his professional and judicial life, shall not be here to speak of it.

Judge Willard was born on the 22d day of May, 1792, at Guilford, Connecticut, and graduated at Middlebury college, in August, 1813. While at college, he was associated with the late Silas Wright and the Hon. Samuel Nelson; men who, like him, rose to offices of high honor and public trust, by the mere force of intellect, united with untiring industry.

To an audience composed of Judge Willard's neighbors, most of whom have had the pleasure of his acquaintance for many years, it would be superfluous to speak of the purity of his private life, of the genuine kindness of his heart, of the mildness and amiability of his disposition. He was generous in all his impulses, warm in his friendships, and sincere in his professions. He was a discreet counsellor, and a wise and judicious adviser; and ever had a pleasant smile and an encouraging word for the younger members of his profession, in whom he always felt a deep interest.

Of Judge Willard's life as a lawyer, a judge and an author, a more extended sketch is due than the present occasion affords. Suffice it to say that he was admitted to the bar in 1817, and commenced practice in Salem, Washington county, where he soon rose to the front rank of his profession. He held the office of surrogate, and subsequently that of first judge of the court of common pleas, of that county, for several years. In 1836, on the promotion of Judge Cowen to the bench of the supreme court, Judge Willard was appointed circuit judge and vice chancellor of the fourth circuit. He soon after removed to this village, and took up his residence among us, and has ever since resided here, a period of more than a quarter of a century. He held the office of circuit judge until it was abolished by the new constitution, in 1847. At the first election under the new constitution, in June, 1847, Judge Willard was elected one of the judges of the supreme court for the fourth judicial district, and held that office for six years, retiring from the bench at the close of 1853. Of his merits as a judge it is unnecessary for me to speak to those who, like you, have had abundant opportunities for personal observation. His manner upon the bench was patient, dignified and courteous. He enjoyed the confidence and esteem of the bar, and his decisions commanded great respect, both at home and abroad. His recorded opinions exhibit great learning and logical ability, and are pervaded by a high-toned morality, and adorned by a lucid style. Among the many able men who have graced the bench of the supreme court, under its present organization, Judge Willard's name occupies a conspicnous place. As an equity judge especially, he stood very high, and his decisions show a great familiarity with the principles of the science.

Upon leaving the bench, Judge Willard—unwilling to waste the remainder of his life in inglorious ease—entered upon a career of authorship, which he pursued with his habitual industry, and which was crowned with great success. In 1855 he published a treatise on Equity Jurisprudence; in 1859, a treatise on Executors, Administrators and Guardians, and, in 1861, a treatise on Real Estate and Conveyancing; and it is understood that at the time of his death he was engaged upon a fourth work, which he probably left unfinished. These are all works of great learning and ability; and have received the stamp of approval from the bench and bar, and the legal reviews, throughout the country. They are every where cited with confidence, and received as authority; and have conferred upon their author an enduring fame. These several works, the results of an unwearied industry, and the fruits of a long and ripe experience, will ever be regarded as a valuable legacy left to his brethren, by one who loved his profession and was proud thus to pay the debt he owed it.

Of his political life it would not be becoming to speak, on this occasion, further than to say that it was straight forward, consistent and honorable, and that he never sought for office, but office sought him, and forced upon him honors which his innate modesty would have prompted him to decline.

Judge Willard, though firm and decided in his political principles, was never an active politician, and declined all offices, except those connected with his profession, until after he had retired from the bench. In the fall of 1861 he was elected to the state senate from this district, and held the office of senator at the time of his death. Of his course in the senate I do not propose to speak, further than to say that he was with his country in her time of peril, and stood by those who were striving to put down this wicked rebellion. In this, as at all other periods of his life, his patriotism rose above party, even at the risk of alienating his life-long friends.

Though in feeble health for some months past, it was hoped that Judge Willard would recover; and it was with painful surprise that his friends learnt, a few days since, that he had been struck down by paralysis. Next we were informed that he was no more. Need I say to you, sir, that we all received this intelligence with deep emotion? It fell upon us with the force of a personal loss. We all felt that we had lost a friend. Indeed, Judge Willard had no enemies. Such high integrity, such kindness of heart, such courtesy of manners could not fail to command the respect and esteem of all.

Such a life, Mr. Chairman, so beautiful and perfect in all its aspects, may well be held up to the young as an example for their admiration—as a model for their imitation. But I feel that I should leave my sketch of it incomplete did I not add that Judge Willard's life was guided by the precepts of the gospel, and his last hours cheered by the hopes of the christian. Having lived the life of faith, he died the death of the righteous, and his reward is with the Most High.

"As the seed which is deposited in the earth decays and dies, and from it springs a plant crested with a beautiful flower, so from its clay tenement which lies dissolved and perished has the pure spirit escaped; but it will live forever, clad in celestial drapery, and crowned with the flowers of heaven."

To us remains the sacred duty of cherishing the memory, and imitating the example of our departed friend.

Nomen in exemplum sero servabimus aevo.

Hon. Judiah Ellsworth said :

Mr. Chairman: I cannot allow these resolutions to pass, by a mere silent assent. Though not within the same circle of intimate familiarity as the chairman and Chancellor Walworth, I knew Judge Willard too well to allow this last chance to speak of his merit to pass without paying a tribute to his memory.

I have known his public judicial character since his accession to the common pleas of Washington county, about 1825. Long before I knew the man, his administration of justice in his county gave that court a reputation second to no common pleas court in the state. When he was appointed circuit judge and became vice chancellor, on his removal to this place, I became well acquainted with Judge Willard, personally. By practice in the supreme court and court of chancery, I became well acquainted with him as a judge.

Judge Willard's moral perceptions were of a rare order, and had been cultivated to a degree of perfection rarely equaled, and he never failed, in common conversation as well as in his action on the bench, to urge on the bar that their duty was to aid the court in reaching the justice of the case. This seemed to be his leading desire—not to shape his action so much by the laws written on paper, as by that law written on the heart. Judge Willard was a model lawyer.

J. A. SHOUDY, Esq., spoke substantially as follows :

Mr. Chairman : As one of the younger members of the profession of which Judge Willard was so bright an ornament, I beg to add one word as my feeble tribute of respect to the memory of the lamented dead.

From the time I began the study of law, I have known him. Commencing my studies in an office adjoining his, where I was frequently called to be in his office and see him there, it has been my privilege to know him better than has been the fortune of most of my brethren of my age. And I can truly say, Mr. Chairman, that I never knew that other man for whose character as a lawyer and a man, I had such profound respect.

It has been truly said that he was the friend of young lawyers. For such, he always had a kind and encouraging word. He pointed them to the higher and nobler walks of the profession—taught them to eschew technicalities, and aim at the right investigation of truth.

The benefit of his example to the profession can hardly be over estimated.

Sir, I have always considered myself fortunate in having been permitted to know and love such a man.

JAMES P. BUTLER, Esq., said :

Mr. Chairman : Those who have addressed the bar on this occasion have been long personally acquainted with the distinguished man whose death we have met to deplore.

It was never my good fortune to know Judge Willard intimately, in the relations of social life. I have known him only in his professional character. I can therefore speak of him as one who has beheld him from a distance ; from such a stand-point you can calculate his dimensions.

The first time I ever entered a circuit court while in session, Judge Willard presided. I was a mere boy. A cause was on trial of very great importance. Excellent counsel were arrayed, Hunt and Ross on one side, and Simmons and Gardiner Stow on the other. These able advocates had discussed the various points with the eminent learning and ability for which they were distinguished. I shall ever remember the clear and lucid style in which Judge Willard, on that occasion, unraveled the entangling questions at issue.

I have always viewed him since that event as a bright and brilliant luminary—"a light set upon a hill "—a sun without a spot—giving light and heat. The shadow into which he has entered cannot dim that light. The grave cannot extinguish his fame.

When the members of the bar of this village shall accompany his earthly remains to the last resting place, we shall look down into the sepulchre of no ordinary man.

It was moved, that the different addresses made upon this occasion, together with the resolutions, be published in the village papers. Carried.

RESOLUTIONS

OF THE

Senate of the State of New York,

INCLUDING

ADDRESSES OF SENATORS CLARK, FOLGER, TOBEY,
MURPHY, COOK AND PRUYN.

In the *State Senate*, of which the deceased was a member, the following proceedings occurred, at the next meeting of that body, on the 9th of January, 1863 :

Mr. CLARK announced the death of the late Hon. John Willard, and said :

Mr. President: It is my painful duty to announce to the senate the death of one of our most worthy members. Senator Willard died at his residence at Saratoga Springs, August 31st, 1862, at the age of 70 years. He died, as he had always lived, respected by all for his many virtues. Senators associated with him are, I understand, prepared to do justice to his memory. In accordance with the usual custom, I offer these resolutions :

Resolved, That in the death of Hon. John Willard the senate has lost an able and faithful member, the country an enlightened statesman, and society an honest man. That with our regrets at the loss to the senate, the country and society, we mingle our sympathy with the bereaved family of our late distinguished fellow senator, and in token of our respect to his memory, recommend that each senator and officer of the senate wear crape on the left arm for one week.

Resolved, That a copy of these resolutions be sent to the family of the deceased.

Resolved, That a copy of the above resolutions be communicated to the Assembly.

3

The question being on the adoption of the resolutions, Mr. Folger addressed the senate as follows:

Mr. President: It seems appropriate that I, as chairman of that standing committee of this house, of which the deceased senator was the ornament and the strength, should second these resolutions.

The announcement just made by the senator from the 15th, is but the utterance of the thought which has been with us all from the opening of this session. In all the greetings and pleasurable excitement of our meeting again, and in the routine of the few days' business, the reflection has ever pressed upon us that one seat has, in the interim, been vacated by death, and that the most venerable, and most experienced and wisest of our body, has gone before us.

It scarcely becomes me to assume to speak, from personal knowledge, of the character of the departed senator, for I never knew him until we met upon committee; and through all the last session I but once saw him elsewhere than in this chamber, or in the committee room. What I knew of him is from his public life, and the inference which I may draw from it. But, Mr. President, dying at his three score years and ten, he dies well, of whom a fitting, a glowing and an ample eulogy is found in the simple narration of the chief events of his life, and whose character can be traced with praise, well marked in the public records of his state.

His life has been chiefly spent in the discharge of judicial duties. The manner of the discharge of them has shown his admirable mental qualifications. The length of his continuance in the office of judge, and the repeated calls of him to that office, show the confiding appreciation of the public, and prove that he possessed not only intellectual ability but high personal character and integrity. For over thirty years, in the same community, he sat upon the bench. He was successively surrogate and first judge of the court of common pleas for nearly twenty years; he was then circuit judge and vice chancellor for ten years, and then justice of the supreme court for six years. In this long occupation of judicial position he was exactly in the focus of the acute and searching intellect of the bar, from which escapes undetected no weakness of the head, and in full view of the people, whose criticism of moral qualification and character is not, in the long run, apt to err. And when judicial labor was ended, he forgot not the debt which, Lord Coke says, every lawyer owes to his profession, but in his learned leisure added to the literature of the law, works which, felicitous and perspicuous in style, and accurate and profound in legal research and learning, are cited in the courts as authoritative text books.

And as a culminating evidence of his eminent qualifications and character, when, in 1861, the people of his district, under the shadow of a peril which hushed party strife and aspirations, looked for a pure man and a wise legislator to represent them in this senate, they spontaneously and with one accord delegated him.

Surely, he was in private a man pure in spirit, blameless in life, upright in heart; and in public, profound in knowledge, signal in ability, steadfast in integrity.

And then he came and met with us, weak in frame and strong in intellect, rich in acquisition, assiduous in duty, never rising in his place but to command the respectful attention of the senate. His labors here were well directed and fructified, and order was restored to the confused state of the law touching the punishment for capital offenses, and the rights of married women, and the relations of husband and wife.

His services in committee, though quiet and unobtrusive, were in the highest degree valuable, for his discrimination and legal learning, ever at command, were the ready touchstone to separate the useful from the needless, and to forestall much painful research. And it was produced with a courtesy and simplicity of manner, and modesty of demeanor, that savored only a wish to aid, not at all of a desire to shine.

Such, in my estimation, was the senator whose death we now memorize. And although with his infirmities of the flesh, and bereft, as he was, of wife and child, and at his age, having stepped far towards the mark beyond which years are but sorrow and trouble, he might well speak of himself, in the language of the heathen poet, as one "who reckoned the close of his life among the boons of nature," (*qui spatium vitæ extremum inter munera ponat, naturæ*,) yet we, as individuals, as citizens and as legislators, cannot but deplore his removal from among us.

Mr. TOBEY said:

Mr. President: The memory of the virtuous and distinguished dead is entitled to a tribute of respect from the living; but independent of the claims of gratitude, to our acknowledgment of the merit and valuable public services of those who have gone before us, past companionship with and friendship for the departed senator, whose death has just now been so appropriately announced by his successor, would prompt me to attempt an expression of my feelings of respect for his memory and of my appreciation of his great worth. His age gave him rank as the Nestor of the senate, while the correctness of his judgment gave point and eminence to the distinction. His unobtrusive merit was shrouded by a modesty that sometimes overshadowed his superior intelligence, until drawn aside by the encouragements of friendship or the necessities of his position. Those only who saw much of the workings of his mind and heart understood the man, or could rightly estimate his value.

It was my fortune to have known him many years, and I witnessed his progress to professional distinction, until he won by his ability the highest judicial honors, laid aside only to assume, at the bidding of the people who knew him best, the duties of a legislator, which he continued to discharge until summoned before the great Sovereign on high. I saw much of him during the last winter, while a member of this body; we dwelt under the same roof, met at the same board, often at the same fireside, and labored on the same committee. His intercourse with men was marked by a kindness of manner that won esteem, and a frankness that secured confidence and commanded respect. Gifted with a memory of more than ordinary strength, he was ever ready to share from its stores treasures of knowledge, ripened into wisdom, dispensing them for the benefit and pleasure of those around him. He had read much, and with discrimination; always a student, he was conversant with the sciences, the classics and the literature of the day. He had within himself and in his books sources of mental enjoyment that compensated for the absence of society when friends were not near; and his virtuous habits withheld him from obtruding upon, while he did not avoid, the company of his acquaintances. He communed much with himself, and thought much for the advantage of others; and the community are now enjoying the fruits of his literary labors. He was born in New England. He was bred to the law in this state, where he resided for about half a century. He loved his profession for the sake of it, and pursued its study with untiring zeal. He laid the ground-work of future professional eminence, by diligently reading the works of those ancient lawyers, whose genius and labors reduced the common law to a system. Possessed of strong sense and a logical mind, cultivated, stored with learning, he became prominent among the judges of the day, and his opinions were reputed for their ability—the research and uprightness of purpose by which they were distinguished. In 1853 he retired from the bench, after having occupied a seat, as judge, for more than thirty years. During that long period, and out of the multitude of cases that came before him, there were doubtless many in which some were dissatisfied with his decisions, but none where his integrity was questioned.

Accustomed to labor, his active mind could not remain idle. When his judicial labors ceased, he felt that it was the duty of every one to contribute in some way to the advantage or happiness of those around him ; and, turning to his books—to him a source of pleasure—he became the author of two learned works, that bear the prefix of his name, which are and will continue to be found in the library of every lawyer, an enduring evidence of the learning, industry and patient research of their author.

In politics, Judge Willard was a democrat ; but when the flag of rebellion was raised, and the stars and stripes were hauled down, his politics were forgotten in his love of country, and he cheered her friends by his advice and countenance, and threw all his influence on the side of the government, the constitution and the laws. In the fall of 1861 he was elected to the senate, and one year ago he took his seat with us as a member of this body, and cheerfully lent his voice and his vote on all occasions to sustain the sovereignty of the union and to crush out the rebellion.

Appointed a member of the committee on the judiciary, he was faithful and diligent in the discharge of the duties of his situation, bringing to the aid of that body his large experience and great learning, avoiding no responsibility, but cheerfully discharging every duty imposed by his position, esteeming no labor too great, no task too arduous, by which the burthen of his associates might be relieved and the initiatory work of legislation could be properly prepared and successfully accomplished.

On the floor, he seldom occupied the time or attention of the senate, but whenever he addressed this body there was no member who was listened to with more respect, nor any whose opinions received more consideration or whose reasons were more convincing. He did not aspire to distinction in debate, but contented himself with the discharge of the legitimate duties of a legislator, in preparing and perfecting laws for the action of the senate, and securing their final passage.

The success of other members has been more brilliant, but there are none whose labors have been more useful to the state, or who has established for himself a reputation more enduring or more enviable.

The severities of our criminal code and the apparent injustice of some of its provisions, had been brought to his notice during a long judicial career, and he successfully strove to procure their modification by amendments which now appear upon our statute book, a monument to his humanity and wisdom, conferring credit upon the intelligence of the legislature by whom they were adopted.

The constitution of Judge Willard was never strong. Long years and severe labor had told upon his physical energies. His health failed before the close of the last session, and he left this scene of his labors never to return. His strength continued to fail during the summer, but his mind and pen were ever active. The last days of his life were devoted to the preparation of an elaborate and valuable report, upon an important subject that had been referred to him by this body, and which, it is expected, will ere long be presented to the senate.

I have not, in these few remarks, sought to do more than refer to the life and labors of our lamented associate, hoping that some competent pen will hereafter do justice, in an enduring form, to that estimable citizen, the learned jurist, the true patriot and enlightened legislator, John Willard.

Mr. MURPHY said:

It was unnecessary, Mr. President, after the just and appropriate terms in which the mournful event which has happened among us has been announced here, for me to add any thing more; and yet I should do injustice to my own feelings if I were to be altogether silent. The announcement was not unexpected. The infirm condition in which the deceased senator left us before the close of the last session, and the advanced age which he had reached, even the allotted life of man, led me to fear, and I doubt not, also, the other members of this body, that we should never meet him again in our circle. He has gone from us forever; and while we submit, on this occasion, to the inexorable law of our nature, which declares that it is appointed unto all men once to die, and humbly bow to the will of Almighty God in this dispensation, we are permitted, nevertheless, to deplore the loss and commemorate the virtues of our friend. The profound learning of the deceased, which has been so justly dwelt upon by the senator from the 11th, (Mr. Tobey,) his pure and unsullied character, his quiet and gentle manners, his devoted patriotism, these, added to his venerable appearance, stamped him in the minds of all those, whether within or without this body, who admire intelligence, wisdom and dignity in that capacity, as, indeed, a senator. Like the senator of the 26th, (Mr. Folger,) my personal acquaintance with Judge Willard commenced with our connection with this body; but some circumstances in common, attending our election to the senate, led me into frequent consultation with him upon many of the important questions which agitated our counsels during the last session. It was in these private interviews that I learned to admire his powers of mind, his profound erudition, his simplicity of character and his ardent patriotism; and, as it were, at his knees to draw lessons of wisdom. He threw always a flood of light upon every subject which came before him —

" Nihil tetigit quod non ornavit."

His loss is a loss not only to this body, but to the state and nation; and while we recall his presence amongst us as adding consideration and strength to our counsels, let the remembrance of his virtues, senators, stimulate us to a conscientious discharge of our duties here, to the welfare of our commonwealth and the peace and concord of our distracted country.

Mr. COOK said:

Mr. President: My relations with the late Judge Willard were such that they may excuse me before the senate, for adding my testimony to that which has been so well and so properly said.

I had known the deceased for many years; but he resided in the northeast and I in the southeast portion of the state; our acquaintance was more of a general than of a personal character; and perhaps it could not be truly said that any confiding personal relations existed between us, until we met here at the commencement of the last session of the senate, to take the oath and our seats as senators of this body.

It then so happened that we had both taken lodgings at the same hotel, and our rooms opened out upon the same hall; and as it was my duty, he being my senior, I called early at his room to pay my respects; that call was promptly returned, and from that time scarcely a day passed that we were not in each other's room, where we discussed various questions that were to come before the senate, in order to determine in our own minds, our representative duties in regard to them.

As others have told you, in early life he turned his attention to the study of the law; and in the profession of the law his labors continued through life, and I have seldom met a man more familiar with the doctrine of rights under the common law, or when and where that law had been broken in upon by statutory provisions; or when the law in any given case was regarded as settled. He appeared to be as well informed of the adjudications in the higher English courts, and the courts of the several states in this union, as he was familiar with the adjudications of our own state.

After one of these evenings of familiar conversation, I have often thought of that distinguished and somewhat peculiar branch of the profession that had grown up in the northern part of this state, eminent for their legal learning and ability, of which the late Judge Cowen, Daniel Cady, Chancellor Walworth, Judge Willard, and the late Nicholas Hill, were among the most distinguished members. All of these have now passed away, except the Chancellor, and whether there remains in that portion of the state those that will make their places good in the profession, future developments of time must determine.

The deceased, like the late Nicholas Hill, had more vigor of mind than strength of body; therefore under the strong and constant workings of the former, the latter yielded; and when, near the end of the last session, failing health compelled him to leave for his home, I think but few senators expected that they would ever see him again in his seat in this senate.

It will be remembered, that the deceased introduced a bill at the last session of the senate, in relation to the old chancery fund of this state, which at one time was said to amount to about three millions of dollars, and now to less than two millions of dollars. When that bill came up for consideration, it was, upon his own motion, referred to the judiciary committee, of which he was a member, to investigate and report at the next session of the senate. This duty the committee referred solely to the deceased.

While at Saratoga for a short time, last summer, I called and spent an evening at his house; was shown into the back parlor, a room plain but neatly furnished, and the portraits of himself and deceased wife were the only paintings that seemed to be allowed upon its walls. It was quite evident that he occupied this room for his evening reading. He appeared quite well, for him, and said he believed he had fully recovered from the succession of colds taken while in Albany during the winter. Among the subjects of our conversation, he early spoke of his report on the old chancery fund; said he had the second draft of it nearly completed, and proposed to read it to me; but being pressed for time, I said no; you will bring it with you to Albany, it will then be published by the senate as the report of the committee, and then we will all see it. He then stated the view he had taken of the question, the power of the legislature over this fund, the practice of the British government, and recalled the period when that government first assumed the control over funds paid into court. But he is not here to present that report; yet the importance of the subject leads us to hope that the other members of that committee will possess themselves of it, that it may come into the keeping of the senate; not only that we may all be informed and benefited by his examination of the question, but also that the senate may be the depository of the last public labors of his official life; and here I may be excused for saying, that upon the coming in of that report, I think enough will be shown to justify the early consideration and the early action of the senate upon the subject of these funds, as it is quite probable that Chancellor Walworth is now the only person living that could give reliable information in regard to them, of whom Judge Willard often said that these funds "were well taken care of while within the chancellor's control;" but, to use his own modest language, "since that time they have not been cared for as they ought to have been." My own impression is, that we ought to feel grateful that our attention has been called to the condition of these chancery funds.

In early life, upon profession of faith, Judge Willard connected himself with the Presbyterian church, and honored that profession by a well ordered life, and was doubtless better prepared at its close for the great change that awaited him than some of us, his associates, in the senate.

Mr. Pruyn said:

Mr. President: Like the senator who has just addressed you, I feel that there are a few thoughts to which I must give utterance. It so happened that I was the only member of this body who was present at the funeral of Judge Willard, and heard the quiet, clear and feeling address of his pastor, portraying his character and virtues. I accompanied the relatives and friends to the grave, and saw deposited in its mother earth the remains of the lamented dead, there to rest until "the resurrection of the just."

Let me say a word as to one or two points in the character of the deceased, which have not been as distinctly presented as others.

As a judge, he was eminently fearless. He knew and thoroughly appreciated his position and duty, and also the place and province of the jury, and he never hesitated to perform that duty, or sought to cast the responsibility of it upon others. How much many of the judges of the present day falter under such circumstances, and its lamentable effect in promoting litigation, the members of the legal profession well know.

Judge Willard was a sincere and devout christian. His tastes were pure, simple and scholarly. His Greek testament was his constant companion, and while expounding the laws of man, he constantly drew strength from the higher law he carried with him, searching the scriptures, for in them he knew were the words of eternal life.

His illness was brief and his death quiet, and it was not long between his being very easy in this world and very happy in the next.

The resolutions were unanimously adopted.

PROCEEDINGS

OF THE

Assembly of the State of New York,

CONTAINING

ADDRESSES BY MESSRS. BROCKETT, HOUGHTON, MOULTON,
McSHEA, REDINGTON, SEYMOUR, HAVENS,
HEACOCK AND POST.

The resolutions of the *Senate* having been communicated to the *Assembly*, they were considered in that body on the fifth day of February, 1863, when

Mr. BROCKETT spoke as follows:

Mr. Speaker: A few days since a resolution of the Senate was communicated to this House announcing the death of Senator Willard. Owing to the peculiar condition of affairs at that time it was laid upon the table, not as an act of disrespect to the memory of the honored deceased, but to await a more favorable time for action. I now call for the resolution, and ask unanimous consent of the House that it may be read. Granted.

The resolutions were then read, as follows, on motion of Mr. CLARK:

Resolved, That in the death of Hon. John Willard the senate has lost an able and faithful member, the country an enlightened statesman, and society an honest man. That with our regrets at the loss to the senate, the country and society, we mingle our sympathy with the bereaved family of our late distinguished fellow senator, and in token of our respect to his memory, recommend that each senator and officer of the senate wear crape on the left arm for one week.

Resolved, That a copy of these resolutions be sent to the family of the deceased.

Resolved, That a copy of the above resolutions be communicated to the Assembly.

Mr. Brockett, after the reading of the resolutions, continued :

Mr. Speaker : I move that the resolutions be concurred in, and upon that motion I desire to make a few remarks.

The resolutions which have been transmitted by the Senate to this House, and which have just been read, communicated to us the painful intelligence of the death of Senator Willard—which melancholy event took place at his residence at Saratoga Springs, August 31, 1862. The deceased Senator had reached the advanced age of seventy years, and during his long and eventful life he held many high and important offices in the State of New York; the duties of which he discharged with that ability, purity and dignity of character, and strict impartiality, which won for him the confidence and respect of all who knew him. He died at a patriarchal age, full of years, and of honors, beloved and esteemed by all who had the pleasure of knowing him—leaving his name impressed on the annals of our jurisprudence in characters of living light. As a resident of the county which Senator Willard so ably and faithfully represented in the Senate of this state, I consider it proper for me to move that the Assembly concur in these resolutions of respect to the deceased senator. I shall, therefore, leave to other gentlemen who are to follow me to do full justice to his memory.

Mr. Houghton spoke as follows :

Mr. Speaker : It is with feelings replete with deep emotion, that I rise to add my humble but heartfelt tribute to the memory of the deceased. I have the honor to represent a portion of the district which was represented by him in the other branch of this legislature. I had a still greater honor. I had the honor of a personal acquaintance with the illustrious Senator—the wise jurist, the unwavering patriot, the true Christian—whose death has been announced to this House. Yes, all that was mortal of the Hon. John Willard has departed; but the light of his example is with us, and points us to the path of rectitude, honor and patriotism—saying, in language more eloquent than words, "Live as I have lived," and you, too, may "make your lives sublime, and departing, leave behind you foot-prints in the sands of time." The venerable judge has gone from the courts of earth to the courts of heaven; from the fallible chancery of mortals to the in-

fallible—the infinite. The patriot has gone to wear the crown of loyalty, and to sit at the right hand of our God.

While it is almost strange that the deceased had so few errors, it
would have been strange, indeed, had he been other than a good man,
for he was descended from the glorious old Pilgrim sires. He was a
son of New England, nurtured in the faith of the fathers—that faith
which taught its votaries that there was but one path to true greatness; that was honor, virtue and true patriotism. In political faith
he was a democrat. But, alas! the recreancy and corruption of political parties was a source of grief and sorrow to the aged hero.
When this rebellion rose, with the torch and ax of civil strife, and
threatened our national life, this venerable democrat rose at once, in
all the dignity of his noble manhood, above all party or political consideration, and said, in the language of the inflexible old hero, Andrew
Jackson, that "our country must be saved and the union preserved."

The late senator occupied official positions connected with the judiciary of this state for nearly forty years. He performed the high
and responsible duties of this position, during this long period of time,
with great honor and credit to himself and to the entire satisfaction
and approval of the varied communities in which he was called to
preside. In the year 1856, he was appointed by President Pierce
one of the commissioners to examine as to the validity of the California land titles. This, as you all know, was a long, laborious and
responsible task. He performed it as he had all other duties that de-
volved upon him, fearlessly, honestly and satisfactorily to the government which had selected him to the performance of the difficult and
important duty. He has left behind him three voluminous tomes;
enduring monuments of his research, industry and application as a
jurist, scholar and commentator. When I allude to his social worth
it should be with head bowed in veneration; for when we contem-
plate his social and Christian virtues, it may well be said of him, as it
was of another, that "the Christian outshone the scholar, the philan-
thropist, the statesman, the patriot, the politician." He loved humanity for humanity's sake. Wherever he beheld her bleeding
wounds, he at once resorted to all judicious means within his reach to
assuage her sufferings and correct her wrongs.

A few months ago the great and good man whose death has produced grief and mourning in every community in which he was ever
known, was a conspicuous member in the co-ordinate branch of this
Legislature. Never, sir, shall I forget his appearance as I beheld

him there in his seat, his very countenance shadowing forth the high and holy thoughts that pervaded his pure and exalted mind. But we have beheld his mortal form for the last time; we shall see his face no more, forever; but his good deeds, his Christian precepts, and the hallowed influences he shed around him will never die.

> " These shall resist the empire of decay
> When time is o'er and worlds have passed away :
> Cold in the dust the perished heart may lie,
> But that which warmed it once can never die."

And I doubt not he looks down from his starry abode upon the country he loved so well and served so faithfully, and his illumined spirit joins in that mighty voice which echoes back to us from the venerable dead, which admonishes and commands us to be true to the trust which they have left us—to preserve, if possible, our country unbroken, our liberties unimpaired, our faith in God unshaken.

Mr. MOULTON spoke as follows :

I do not know that I ought to add a single poor word of mine to the eloquent remarks of my colleagues who have preceded me. But, Mr. Speaker, the humblest follower in a funeral pageant may throw a simple flower on the grave of one whom he loves or reveres. My first recollection of the distinguished citizen, jurist and statesman, whose loss we deplore, was when as the distinguished justice of the Supreme Court of my own judicial district, he presided, with grace and judicial impartiality, over the circuit of my native county. The records of his legal labors are found in every volume of law reports in our state. But, sir, it was the last efforts of his life that will cause his memory to be embalmed in the hearts of his countrymen so long as patriotism shall be cherished by the American people. Stirred by the dangers which threatened his loved country, he left his long sought for and much coveted retirement, devoting all the powers of his well disciplined mind, all the faculties which God and nature had given him, to unite his fellow citizens in putting down this monstrous and unnatural rebellion.

Mr. Speaker: Few upon the floor of this house may expect to arrive at the distinction or acquire the fame of the deceased senator. But, sir, we may all walk in the path his footsteps have hallowed : we may emulate him in his love of country and in offering upon its altar all love of party, all preconceived partisan prejudices, if, by so doing, we may assist in the smallest degree in saving our country from the horrible death which so slowly yet so surely seems to await it.

Mr. McShea spoke as follows:

Mr. Speaker: After the eloquent and appropriate manner in which the gentlemen who have preceded me have spoken of the late lamented Senator WILLARD, it may, perhaps, be considered unnecessary for me to add any thing to what they have so well and so beautifully said on this occasion. But, as the representative of an adjoining county to that in which Judge WILLARD lived and died, and a resident of the same congressional district, in behalf of the people whom I have the honor to represent, by whom he was well known and highly respected, I wish to add my humble mite to the tribute of respect which has been this day so justly paid to his memory.

It is right and proper to commemorate the virtues and patriotism of the honored dead, more particularly in this age of corruption in high places, and to point them out as proper models for the respect and imitation of the rising generation. Born on the soil of New England—which, with all its isms, has given birth to so many men of pre-eminent genius, whose glowing eloquence and resplendent talents would shed lustre on any land—Senator WILLARD in early life made this state his future home, where he studied law, and lived for more than half a century, beloved and respected by his fellow men, and died at an advanced age, crowned with the honors and rewards of a well-spent life.

During his long and eventful life he was peculiarly honored by the people, who loved him for his many amiable qualities of head and heart, and admired him for his superior knowledge of the law, his disinterested patriotism and integrity of purpose. For nearly twenty years he was successively surrogate and first judge of the court of common pleas. For ten years he discharged the duties of circuit judge and vice chancellor, and for six years was a justice of the supreme court. Such a long continuance in such high and important offices, occupying the exalted position of judge in the same community for more than thirty years, is a more beautiful and appropriate eulogy on the life and character of Judge WILLARD than the most eloquent words could express, and a sufficient proof of the high estimation in which he was so justly held by the intelligent and patriotic people of Saratoga county, who knew him best.

A close and attentive student in early life, he laid the foundation of his after fame by studying the writings of those distinguished men, whose invaluable works on the statute and common laws have rendered their names famous, not only in England, but throughout the length and breadth of this land. He anxiously labored to acquire those literary treasures which adorn the mind, by diligent research and in communion with the great and immortal spirits of the past, who at the toil of anxious hours of thoughtful labor, have coined for us from the golden treasury of their intellects, thoughts more precious than the golden sands of California, bright even as the soldier's lance, imperishable as the patriot's fame, brilliant and beautiful as the emerald's refulgent sheen.

When, in 1853, he retired from the bench, he did not repose in inglorious idleness, but with that desire to benefit his fellow men which had ever characterized his actions, he resolved to give them the benefit of his long experience and extensive knowledge of the law in three volumes, which bear the prefix of his name, which are highly spoken of by the legal profession, and are cited in our courts as authoritative text books.

In politics Judge WILLARD was a democrat, believing that the best interests of his country would be promoted by the success of democratic principles. The first time I ever saw him was as a delegate to the state convention which met in this city just two years ago this month, at which many of the gentlemen whom I see around me were present, and which, I venture to say, contained more men of venerable appearance and intelligence than ever before assembled in a state convention, the object of which was, if possible, to preserve peace and avert this dreadful civil war which has brought suffering to thousands of firesides and dyed the green fields of our country with the best blood of our sons. When civil war was inaugurated, and a deadly blow struck at the government, under which he had been born and lived for nearly three-quarters of a century, like many others, with him party became merged in patriotism, and he gave his support to those in power, believing them to be then actuated by an earnest desire to restore the Union and maintain the constitution in all its purity and entirety, just as it came from beneath the hands of the immortal Father of his country.

In 1861, when the fierce contentions of party were for a time hushed in view of the impending gloom of war which, like a pall, over-shadowed the land — when ability, integrity and patriotism were considered especially necessary in a representative—the people of Saratoga county selected Judge Willard to represent them in the state senate. His actions as a legislator are, I suppose, known to you all. No member of the senate was more attentive to his legislative duties, or more faithful in their discharge. As a member of the judiciary committee his services were considered invaluable by his colleagues in the senate, not only in the initiatory measures of legislation, but in maturing and perfecting them. His long administration of our criminal code, and his thorough knowledge of our laws, made him perfectly acquainted with their defects; and his humane disposition induced him to procure their amendment so as to make them more in accordance with the spirit of the age, and to blend justice with mercy. He also made many necessary changes in the laws with regard to the rights of married women, and established on a juster and more equitable basis the relations between husband and wife.

He was a man of refined tastes and enlarged views—studious, thoughtful and reflecting—possessing a cultivated mind, adorned with the rich and beauteous garniture of classic erudition, which in his leisure hours he had carefully culled from the choicest authors, ancient and modern. What a delicious mental banquet he there found before him! How many fountains of knowledge were unsealed, sending forth their pellucid and invigorating streams to satiate his thirst for knowledge! A silent monitor there pointed out to him the path to future honor, usefulness and fame, as he drew from the sacred fount of knowledge the portion of its crystal waters requisite for his walk in life. He loved education for its intrinsic loveliness and worth, for he knew that it was bright and beautiful as the stars, and that like the orb of day its golden effulgence encircled the globe. And in the evening of life he was well repaid for his hours of youthful study by the knowledge that he had been enabled faithfully and properly to discharge the duties of the high offices he had been honored with by the people, and had besides a large fund of knowledge upon which to draw for enjoyment.

Others may have exhibited more shining qualities—may have been more brilliant and attractive, but few have left behind a brighter or more glorious record in the public service, or a proud or more enviable reputation among his fellow-men. Like many other distinguished men, he was unassuming, plain and unostentatious in his manners: but had, withal, a certain air of quiet dignity, which, while it won respect, prevented impertinent intrusion. But the crowning and most beautiful part

5

of his character was that high moral tone which permeated all his actions; refining, elevating and ennobling every thought and deed—leaving its impress on all his actions, stamping them with the nobility of true greatness. The brightest intellect, the most resplendent talents, without this governing and directing moral influence, may prove injurious to their possessor and the community; but when to brilliant endowments is added a pure and high toned morality, directing and guiding them in accordance with the eternal principles of truth and justice, then we behold a truly great man. Such a man was Senator Willard.

His death is a loss to the state and nation at this time, as we require men like him of experience, of wisdom, possessing the confidence and respect of their fellow men, and imbued with genuine patriotism, to carry us through this perilous crisis in the history of our country. He was one of a class getting too few in numbers for the good of our country. Men of a superior mould, giants in thought and language, the coruscations of whose genius shed a halo of glory around the age in which they lived, and reflect credit on the land of their birth—men, venerable for their years, their eminent abilities and exalted patriotism, upon whose heads have rested honors more prized by freemen, than the diadem which decks the brow of royalty. Like the kingly oaks of the forest, over whose giant limbs the winds of heaven had passed for a century, they stood proudly pre-eminent among their fellow men; but one by one they are falling, covered with the snows of age, and amid the regrets of a grateful people whom they had so long loved and served!

Born in the morning of the young republic, he witnessed with pride its growing power and greatness, until it had attained a proud pre-eminence among the nations of the earth. He saw it increase in population, in wealth, in manufactures, and in all the arts and sciences which constitute national greatness, with a rapidity never before witnessed in ancient or modern times. Its territory, stretching from the Atlantic to the golden shores of the Pacific, embracing every variety of soil and climate, forming thirty-four sovereign, independent states, the grandest, the noblest confederacy this world ever saw. And it must have caused him sincere sorrow before his death to witness it engaged in a civil war and almost in the throes of dissolution; for his love of country was so great that, like the celebrated Grecian lawgiver, if his expatriation from the land of his birth, which he dearly loved, would have preserved the liberties of his country and maintained the union, he would cheerfully have made the sacrifice.

In ancient times they apotheosized their great men, and built statues and temples in their honor; but our distinguished men need no such things to perpetuate their memories. Their names and deeds are a portion of our history, and the highest honor we can pay them is to practice their noble and unselfish patriotism, and do all in our power to restore that union which was the pride of their youthful days and the bright heritage they had hoped to have left to their children. Let us bury our divisions and dissensions, and promise over the graves of our noble dead to reconstruct if possible our heretofore glorious union on a firm and immovable basis, and on the ruins of our past contentions we will erect a new and glorious temple of liberty, in which shall be inscribed in letters of living light the names of the patriarchs of freedom, the heroes and sages who founded this republic, and also of those who preserved it from destruction; and there, on the tablet of fame, will appear the name of John Willard, the accomplished scholar, the profound lawyer, the impartial judge and distinguished senator.

Mr. REDINGTON spoke as follows:

Mr. Speaker: My acquaintance with the late Judge WILLARD induces me to intrude upon the attention of the House but for a few moments. In the earlier days of my life, and when I had but just entered upon the duties of my profession, Mr. WILLARD was appointed circuit judge of the judicial district of which St. Lawrence county forms a part. In discharging the duties of his office, almost the first thing that attracted my attention was his kindness and urbanity to the younger members of the bar. Always ready and willing to give the most earnest attention to the remarks and suggestions of the more feeble and younger members of the profession, I can never forget his calm and placid countenance as he presided in court, and with what ready access he was approached by all alike, without regard to fame or distinguished position. His decisions, though with unmistakable firmness, were always without offense, and marked with the most unsullied integrity. I early learned that he was a true Christian, the evidence of which was exemplified in every act of his life. Although a distinguished jurist, and occupying a very elevated position in this respect, he early acknowledged the power and divinity of Christ. After the lapse of many years, having retired from the profession a little more than twelve months since, I met the Judge here in Albany in the discharge of his legislative duties. He recognized me at once

and gave me a cordial shake of the hand. I then saw or thought I
saw, as I looked upon his venerable countenance and form, that his
lamp of life was nearly extinguished, that his race was nearly run.
Though then in the legislative service of his country, and feeling
deeply anxious, as I well knew that he did, about the dangers and
perils that menaced that country, I felt that it was to be his last service. What I then thought has proved too true, and he now finds a
peaceful and honored grave. If our country is to be broken into
fragments, and we made a byword and a reproach among the nations
of the earth, his eyes can never behold it. If our glorious Union,
formed by the patriotism of our fathers, is to be broken into pieces;
if our flag, the emblem of our country's greatness and glory, is to be
trampled upon and despised; if we, like the poor Pole, are obliged to
wander about without a home or a country, his heart can never be
pained by it.

Mr. Speaker: This life is a dream. Though we may live our allotted time of three score years and ten, yet life is like the weaver's shut-
tle, each advancing year seems to grow shorter and shorter as we
approach the hour that lays us with the dead. Happy will it be for
me, sir, for you, and for every member of this honorable body, if our
lives are as pure as the eminent man whose name I am now attempt-
ing to eulogize. Imbued with his pure principles of Christianity, we
may indeed finally hope to enter upon that eternal and happy future
where death never enters. And when the storms and troubles of this
life are over, when we have passed over the excitements and passions
of the hour, when our political differences are forever ended, and when
the places that now know us in this Assembly chamber, and in time,
shall know us no more forever — I say imbued with his pure principles of Christianity we may indeed hope to be anchored with him and
by him in that haven of everlasting rest, where no storm ever enters.
That this may finally be our portion is the humble prayer of him who
now addresses you.

Mr. SEYMOUR spoke as follows:

Mr. Speaker: Those resolutions are a proper tribute to a great and
good man. The life and career of Judge Willard form an important
part of the history of our state. As judge and vice-chancellor, under
the old constitution, and subsequently judge in our supreme court
and court of appeals, he gained the highest eminence for his integrity
and accurate judicial learning. He gave dignity and character to the

tribunal of which he was the ornament. His published works and decisions are a proud monument to his fame as a lawyer and jurist. In the Senate he proved himself a faithful and able legislator.

Thus, one by one, amid our national calamities, are passing away the great lights that have guided us in the past, leaving only their noble teachings and bright example. His long and honorable life, his calm and triumphant departure, renew to us the admonition—

> " So live, that when thy summons comes to join
> The innumerable caravan, that moves
> To that mysterious realm, where each shall take
> His chamber in the silent halls of death.—
> Thou go not, like the quarry-slave at night,
> Scourged to his dungeon, but, sustained and soothed
> By an unfaltering trust, approach thy grave
> Like one who wraps the drapery of his couch
> About him, and lies down to pleasant dreams."

Mr. P. E. Havens spoke as follows :

Mr. Speaker: I do not arise to pronounce an additional eulogy on the life and virtues of the deceased. I concur in all that has been so well and eloquently said by the gentlemen who have preceded me. They have done no more than justice to the illustrious dead.

I had the honor of a personal acquaintance with the deceased, and knew him both as judge and senator. I shall never forget an interview I had with him soon after his election as senator, and which is called fresh to my mind by the remarks that have just been made. He alluded to his long and arduous labors in public life, from which he had retired in hope to spend his declining years in peace and quiet: but the dangers that threatened our beloved country had induced him again to surrender the blessings of home and private life, to obey his country's call in its hour of peril: and give the remaining energies of his life in efforts to protect and save that country from the horrors of secession. And, while a tear glistened in his eye, he remarked that if he could but live to see the flag of our union again wave over an undivided nation, he should be ready to depart in peace.

Sir, we have lost too many of those noble patriots since the rebellion broke out, who have seemed to droop and die under the anguish of heart and weight of sorrow occasioned by the national dangers and troubles in which we are involved. In my own town has fallen one who was a cotemporary and an intimate friend of the lamented Judge Willard, and who, during a long professional life, had won the esteem and confidence of his fellow citizens, and was regarded as one of the fathers and supporters of the nation, to whom we could all look for counsel and advice in time of trouble. I refer to the Hon. HENRY H. ROSS, of Essex. Well in the afternoon of life, his spirit, too, was unable to bear up under the gloomy prospect of our country, and he took his leave to that land of rest and peace where cruel war and civil strife was never known.

Mr. Speaker, these great losses to our country should stimulate us who remain to still greater efforts to meet the increased responsibility thus thrown upon us, in this "time which tries men's souls."

Mr. HEACOCK said:

Having the honor to represent a portion of the district so ably represented in the Senate by the late Judge WILLARD, it affords me a melancholy pleasure to unite with those who have paid so noble tributes to his memory. I had not the honor of a personal acquaintance; but I am happy to say, here, that his praise is on every tongue in my district. I only add my prediction that his noble character, deeds and worth, will live in the memory of his countrymen long after the marble which marks his resting place shall have crumbled back to dust.

Mr. POST said:

Mr. Speaker: I desire to say but a single word upon these resolutions relative to the lamented Judge WILLARD.

He was at once a man, an incorruptible and wise jurist; and, above that, possessed unquestioned loyalty and patriotism.

4

In Memoriam.

HON. JOHN WILLARD,

OF SARATOGA.

No person, now living, has had equal opportunities with myself of knowing the facts, connected with the whole life and character of the late JOHN WILLARD of Saratoga. It is therefore, that I deem it suitable to give here a brief sketch — not of the idealized portrait of the remarkable man we commemorate, but of his individual features, taken from actual life, and in every-day costume.

My acquaintance with JOHN WILLARD, the nephew and namesake of my deceased husband, commenced in his seventeenth year; two months after he entered Middlebury College in 1809 — where he was placed by his uncle. Thus, during the four years of his college life, he was a member of my family; and I soon regarded him with a confidence, which to the day of his death was never disappointed.

His reliability of character was entire, embracing small things as well as great. His appreciation of time as it passed, exceeded that of any other person I have ever known. Hence his power to attain that extraordinary punctuality, which was ever one of his pre-eminent characteristics. During his college life, the regularly recurring duties of the week, the day,

and the hour, were always remembered in their exact order;
and from settled principles of action, they were never neg-
lected. His impulse was rather to perform them a little
in advance of the time. Thus, like the man who pays his
bills before due, he worked with a cheerful alacrity; and at
the same time with such regulated exercise of body and mind,
as ensures health, by giving to each its due proportion of
employment. In harmony with this happy tone of his educational life, was that innate love of knowledge, which makes
its acquisition delightful.

During the four years of his collegiate course, he never
received a single demerit for absence from recitation, or even
for tardiness; although he roomed and studied at home,—
nearly a quarter of a mile from the old college where he
recited. Ever, as his lesson was learned, he was wont to
descend the stairs from his room to the front hall, and to be
there, walking backward and forward, ready to step out over
the threshold, with the first stroke of the college bell; and
he would be at the recitation room exactly in time; neither
too early—which has its disadvantages—nor by any means
a moment too late.

This exactness of punctuality was not only an important
element in his success as a college student, but being founded
in nature, and cultivated into an unfailing habit, it was a
material element in the eminent success of his whole career.
In social life he never disappointed friends who expected him;
nor as a lawyer did his clients ever have to make fruitless
journeys, to find a man who had forgotten his engagement and
wandered from his office. But it was as a judge, that the
full magnitude of this virtue of our friend was seen. How
much of the time, and the expenses of suitors with their
attendant witnesses was saved, and how much the ends of
public justice were served in his courts by the inflexible punctuality of the judge, may be known by inquiring of the lawyers and suitors who attended; and they will say, that not
only was the judge punctual himself, but that he possessed the
resolute intrepidity of character to bring, quietly, all about

him who were directly or indirectly concerned in the business of his courts, to his own standard of exactness of time.

Intrepidity of character was another of WILLARD's distinguishing traits. It was founded in a calm natural courage, which was never allowed to degenerate into rashness; and in an inherent self-possession which no unexpected circumstances ever discomposed. Thus he was always himself—always ready to act—and with all his faculties about him. But the full dignity of intrepidity of character, implies also another element, which in the mind of WILLARD held supremacy over all his other powers. This was an innate sense of justice, accompanied as it ever is, by truthfulness. And concerning the twofold rule of justice or right—do right and have right—young WILLARD felt its force in both its parts; having never the affectation of the novel-hero, to ignore obligations because due to himself; and thus to disturb the balance of things, by setting generosity before justice. Yet was he kind in his disposition—glad to give—but he must first be certain that what he gave was his own. Generosity he felt had no place, till the supreme law of Justice was first satisfied.

His friends at home were watchful that this high attribute of his nature—the sense of justice, should be improved, and not obscured, by education; being never willing—nor did he desire it—that he should take part in any disputation that required of him to set his words at variance with his belief; thus favoring the dangerous fallacy, that there is an art by which truth may be manufactured—leading to mental habits, which impair morality, and destroy the foundation of true eloquence. He had not, like Daniel Webster, the natural advantages of a commanding figure and an oratorical voice; but he had through life a weight of character, which gave weight to his words. If to convince the understanding and persuade the will be eloquence, then was he eloquent.

WILLARD having passed through the first two years of his college course without a single fault-mark, one of the authority, to prove that he was not partial, allowed a mark to stand against him for tardiness at prayers, which the whole class knew to be undeserved. The next morning the class were startled by the unusual appearance of WILLARD entering the chapel after the preliminary exercises had begun—for which, as he expected, he received a second mark. He made no apology; but having given this quiet intimation, that

" He knew his rights, and knowing dare maintain ;"

he went through the remaining two years of his course without another mark, either for transgression or delinquency. He graduated in 1813.

His college course completed—with the advice of his friends he left Vermont, to study law and seek its honors in a broader sphere. He left us with no outward property but his books of study. We said "John we have high expectations for you ; and nothing will satisfy us, short of your going upon the bench of the Supreme Court of the State of New York." After twenty-three years of devotion to public and private duty, keeping himself meantime unstained from every vice, he rose to the dignity, which from the promise of his early life, his friends had believed him capable of attaining ; and it was the career to which we believed that his youthful indications especially pointed. And as Judge of the Supreme Court, not only did he render great services, but he made himself a model to others. What more valuable educational tract could be put into the hands of a young man than the unvarnished life of the Hon. JOHN WILLARD of Saratoga ?

In 1829 he was married (from my house in Troy) to ELIZA SMITH, the woman of all others best suited to be his wife. Their only child, was a lovely daughter ; whose understanding it was his delight to cultivate, as it was her mother's to superintend her accomplishments,—particularly music. Perfect domestic concord blessed this amiable household ; and dark was the sorrow that overshadowed it, when the beloved daughter was taken away by death. The mother, not well before, never recovered from the shock. She died six years thereafter—late in the autumn of 1859. It was then feared by his friends, that his silent undemonstrated grief, would soon lay him by

the side of his wife and daughter ; and I willingly accepted
his invitation to spend the succeeding winter of 1859–60 with
my friend and relative at his home in Saratoga.

In the house of mourning, the long winter evenings were
spent in uninterrupted conversation. When in his youth,
his course had been to me a pleasant stream ; now it was a
majestic river, whose progress and affluents, it interested me
to learn. Then, with his few college books, he was beginning
to acquire knowledge ; now with his large, well-selected, and
well-read library, he had fulfilled all Bacon's conditions—and
had become the full, the correct, and the ready man. He was
at this time putting his knowledge to a use, which will, I am
persuaded, carry his name and labors to future generations.
He was writing the second of those three large volumes of legal
science, with which he has enriched his country's law literature,
and aided her jurisprudence. And it was owing to his early
habits, that he was thus able to occupy himself in doing good
under the weight of crushing sorrow ; and no doubt his
sorrows were lightened by his engaging, systematically, in
significant employments.

The progress of his authorship was remarkable, considering
the important nature of his works, which were to be used as
authorities in courts of justice, and thus constantly exposed
to the criticism of the most astute. He had no copyist. He
seldom interlined, or rewrote. It was his own manuscript,
with few corrections, that went to his printer. His habit was
to begin writing at a certain hour in the morning, and to leave
off as regularly, before exhaustion should commence.

In our conversations, it was natural that I should love to
inquire how the principles pursued in his education had
affected his course in life. Had he ever found any reason to
doubt the principle upon which we insisted, when he was in
college, that the cultivation of justice in the heart, and truth
in the speech, is the foundation not only of sound morality,
but of all effective eloquence ? He never had—although in
the beginning, as a poor young lawyer getting business slowly,
he had strong temptations. He was sometimes assigned by

courts to defend bad men; but then, his duty only required of him to set forth all the extenuating points in the case. Scoundrels, who deserved punishment, soon learned to keep clear of him. As for such poor fellows, as had been thoughtlessly led into wrong, he would frequently give them advice gratis—often tell them to flee—repent and reform. His character once established, the causes he did get, he almost invariably gained. He plead them in earnest; his conscience being with, and not against him.

The period of his going to Albany to argue his first cause before the supreme court, was especially impressed upon his memory. It was at the time, when that court was so proudly eminent, having Ambrose Spencer at its head. He observed that nothing escaped the penetration of that Judge, and that whenever he had heard a matter explained once, his wrath would kindle, when some long-winded pleader attempted to go over it again. So when WILLARD'S own case came up, and the opposing lawyer had made his statement, he began where his adversary left off; and by a concise and clear exposition of his case, he soon had the earnest attention of the Judge. He then briefly related what proposal of settlement he had made to his opponent; "and" rejoined Spencer, "what *could* they say against that?" He bowed, and begged the court's permission to leave it to the opposing counsel. He won the cause, and eventually the friendship of the judges.

After he became himself a Judge, WILLARD's well-balanced mind was never moved by the phrenzies of the day; hence he was extensively regarded as a tower of defense against popular excesses. Once, as he had been called down the Hudson to decide an anti-rent suit, the party whose cause, though popular was illegal, sent him word that he need not come; they would settle the matter among themselves.

He told me, pleasantly, an anecdote which dates back to the violent days of the Maine liquor law—how he met the extreme conscientiousness of a grand jury, with respect to an innkeeper, who had sold a quart of brandy to be carried, contrary to his license, off his premises; although it was ordered by a surgeon, to bathe the bruises of a wayfaring man who had been thrown from a wagon. " I told them," said the Judge, " why you would have indicted the good Samaritan, for taking care of the man who went down from Jerusalem to Jericho and fell among *thieves.*"

The evidence of that reliability of character which we have claimed for our friend, is found in the fact, that he was trusted, by all men and all classes of men, as far as he was known. In Salem, where he studied law and first opened his office, and in Saratoga, his last sojourn on earth, he had many public trusts to fulfill ; and he ever spent much of his valuable time in giving, gratis, advice in the business affairs of his neighbors and friends—of the helpless widow, and the friendless orphan.

Through life, he had never need to seek for office. When he went upon the bench of the Supreme Court of the State, Gov. Marcy, (who was wont thus to forestall office seekers,) gave him a surprise, by sending him his appointment. But in the manner of his being chosen to the State Senate, there was something, not only honorable to him, but nationally encouraging ; that, in these later days of American degeneracy, the people of his senatorial district should have shown a patriotic wisdom worthy of those good times of our republic, when men were chosen, not because they wanted the office, but because the office wanted them. JUDGE WILLARD had never been a member either of the state or national legislature ; he was engaged in writing law books, and his feeble health required the comforts of home ; but deeply anxious for the fate of his distracted country, when he heard her voice, he obeyed. The voters of his district were divided into three parties. He was nominated by each, and voted for—by all.

When in the legislature, his gray hairs were seen as punctually moving to his morning seat in the senate-chamber, as were the dark-brown locks of his youth, to the recitation hall of Middlebury College. The oldest man in the legislature— there by an extraordinary event—the unanimous call of his whole district—having for thirty years been looked up to, as a Judge, courteous, kind and just—he was now, by his associates, treated with unwonted respect, mingled with filial tenderness. Thus, the Senate, seeking to honor him and avail themselves of his legal ability, placed him on the judiciary committee, expecting of him that he would do the important work of remoddling the criminal law, yet considerately forbearing to tax him with such minor cares as must fall upon the chairman of the committee. In forming the law to amend the criminal code, he was but carrying out, as a legislator, views concerning criminal jurisprudence, which as a judge he had previously matured. The bill reported on the 7th of February, 1862, was, every word, written by his own hand; and both houses passed it without debate. After the adjournment of the Senate, still he was laboring in the business of the committee, at his own house; to form a satisfactory plan for settling the great and difficult question of the chancery fund. The pile of sheets he had written over, he showed me as they lay on his office table the week before he was stricken down. He was pleased with the progress he had made, and confident in the hope that he should have his report completed in season. As the Governor of the state was known to place high value on his judgment, men of his district who were candidates for office, and could show evidence of fitness, resorted to him for recommendations. In giving these, party considerations had no place. Feeble as he then was, it was affecting to see with what cheerfulness and courtesy he listened to their statements, and gave them his advice and assistance. " I owe it to them," he said, " they all voted for me." Thus was he laboring incessantly in the duties of his high station:—and in life's battle he died with his armor on.

In his college days, WILLARD, although he ever treated with profound respect, whatever things or persons appertained to religion, yet he was not then, the devout Christian which he afterwards became; and I took opportunities to draw him out, on subjects connected with the change. To say that a man was converted by the ten commandments, would perhaps create a smile. But his mind, bent on the whole history of law, was struck by the evidence, that at the period of the world when that grand epitome of law was presented,—the Decalogue was above the unaided faculties of man to produce ; and must therefore be ascribed to the immediate agency of God. And in the gospel, he recognized God's sovereign right of mercy, pardoning through a Redeemer, those whom his justice must otherwise condemn. Thus WILLARD meekly trusted ;—and "his flesh doth rest in hope."

EMMA WILLARD.

D '14

www.ingramcontent.com/pod-product-compliance
Lightning Source LLC
Chambersburg PA
CBHW030904260626
47169CB00008B/2684